Franz Kafka (1883–1924) is best known as the author of *The Metamorphosis*, *The Trial* and *The Castle*. He was born in Prague and lived most of his life there, though he travelled in Germany and Austria and took holidays in France and Italy.

Kafka was a highly visual writer and he often drew sketches and doodles. Many of these are cartoon-like and androgynous 'everyman' figures, who express profound emotion through their exaggerated body language and elongated limbs.